WALT DISNEY PRODUCTIONS

presents

SNOW WHITE
Helps the Seven Dwarfs

Random House  **New York**

Book Club Edition
First American Edition. Copyright © 1980 by The Walt Disney Company.
All rights reserved under International and Pan-American Copyright
Conventions. Published in the United States by Random House, Inc.,
New York, and simultaneously in Canada by Random House of Canada
Limited, Toronto. Originally published in Denmark as SNEHVIDE OG DE
7 SMÅ DVAERGE I KNIBE by Gutenberghus Bladene, Copenhagen.
ISBN: 0-394-84808-X (trade); 0-394-94808-4 (lib. bdg.)
Manufactured in the United States of America
          0   C D E F G H I J K

Snow White was a beautiful princess.
She lived with her prince in a castle
high on a hill.
She was very happy.
She spent her days picking flowers...
feeding her pet swans...

and singing with the birds.

But one morning Snow White felt sad.
She thought of the time when she lived
with her friends, the seven dwarfs.
Suddenly she missed them very much.

Snow White went to her husband the prince.

"My dear," she said, "I would like to visit my friends the dwarfs."

"That's a good idea," said the prince. "I will come and get you tonight."

So Snow White packed a basket of food
and headed for the woods.

She knew the dwarfs would be working
in the mine.

She would surprise them when they came
home for dinner!

Snow White walked all morning.
She walked up and down hills.
Once she stopped for a drink of water.

At noon Snow White arrived at the
cottage of the seven dwarfs.

She opened the door and walked in.
What a mess!

"The dwarfs were never very neat,"
Snow White said to herself. "I'll start
cleaning right away."

Snow White cleaned the whole cottage.
Her animal friends helped her.
She scrubbed the floor...

made the beds...

and washed the dishes.

Finally Snow White sat down!
Then she fixed the dwarfs' socks.
And she waited for them to come home.
She thought her friends would be there soon.

Suddenly the sky
got very dark.

It began to rain.

Snow White saw lightning and heard
thunder rumbling in the distance.

The dwarfs were not home yet,
and she was worried.

The dwarfs in the mine
heard the thunder, too.
"We'd better go home
right away," said Doc.

The other dwarfs agreed.
They packed up
their tools.
Doc and Grumpy
stepped out of the
mine first.

Just then a bolt of lightning struck down a big tree nearby.

CRASH!

The tree blocked the entrance to the mine.

Doc and Grumpy were not hurt, but the other five dwarfs were trapped in the mine.

"Humph," said Grumpy. "This will make us late for dinner!"

"Well, dinner must wait. We will have to get them out first," said Doc.

First they all tried to move the tree. But they were not strong enough.

Then Doc and Grumpy tried to chop it with their picks and shovels.

That didn't work, either.

"We will have to go home and get better tools," Doc shouted to the others. "Don't worry. We will be back soon."

Doc and Grumpy started on the long walk back to their cottage.

The storm was getting worse and worse.

"Humph," said Grumpy. "Why did this have to happen?"

"Don't worry," said Doc. "It won't take us long to get them out."

They finally reached the cottage.
A light was on inside.
"Oh dear," said Doc. "Who could be there?"

Quietly they peeked in the window.

"Why, it's Snow White!" Doc said happily.
"Yes," said Grumpy. "But of all days!"

Doc and Grumpy ran through the door.
"Snow White, it's so good you are here,"
said Doc.

"Something terrible has happened. The other dwarfs are trapped in the mine...."

"And we have to get them out!" said Grumpy.

"Don't worry,"
Snow White said.

"Get the tools you will need. I will
make some hot cocoa and sandwiches to
bring along," she said. "You must all
be very hungry."

"Yes," said Doc,
"but the only thing
that matters right
now is getting
the others out."

Soon the three headed back to the mine.
It was still raining, and it was very dark.
They were all wondering how the other
dwarfs were doing.

When they reached the mine, the rain had stopped.

Doc showed Snow White the entrance. It was still blocked by the big tree.

First Doc and Grumpy
tried to push the tree....

Then they tried to pull it with a rope....
But the tree would not move.
Grumpy kicked it in anger.

They did not know
what to do next.

Then they saw
the prince on
his horse.

They called out to him.

The prince was happy to see his wife.

Snow White told him how the big tree fell and trapped five dwarfs in the mine.

Snow White also told the prince how Doc and Grumpy had tried to move the tree.

"Don't worry," said the prince. "I will help you."

He went to his horse and took a rope out of his saddlebag.

The prince tied one end of the
rope to his horse and the other
end to the tree.

Then he told the horse to pull.

Soon the horse pulled the tree
away from the mine.

The dwarfs were free!
Everyone was so happy.
The prince took Snow White in his arms,
and the dwarfs danced around them.

But Grumpy remembered the basket Snow White had brought along.

"It is way past dinnertime," he said, "and we are just dancing around. Where is your basket, Snow White?"

"I brought something, too," said the prince. "Let's have a party."

So they all sat
down and had a
wonderful picnic
in the grass.

The hot cocoa, sandwiches, and fruit tasted so good!

"Hooray for Snow White and the prince!" shouted the seven dwarfs.

When they finished eating,
the prince said to
Snow White, "It is getting
late. We should return to
the castle now or someone
will worry."

The seven dwarfs took off their hats
and waved good-bye.

"Thank you," they called. "Come back soon."

"We will," said Snow White.